# mpaSaurusPotalope

Story by Randall C Haines

Illustrations by Jaci Rice

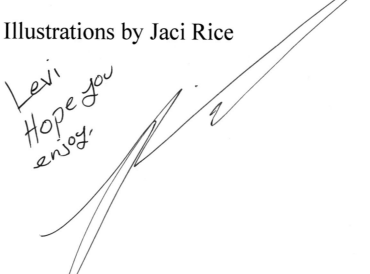

Levi
Hope you
enjoy.

Printed by CreateSpace, An Amazon.com Company

Story Copyright © 2017 Randall C Haines

Illustration Copyright © 2017 Jaci Rice

Printed in the United States of America

ISBN-13: 978-1544889016

ISBN-10: 1544889011

For HARPER and ELLE

R.C.H.

For ELIJAH and EMMA

J.R.

At noon today, you went down for a sleep.
You were supposed to get comfy and not make a peep.

**Instead of sleeping you opted for fun,
And wrestled and played until nap time was done.**

**Now it's late and you're beginning to turn,**
**Into a thing that brings great concern.**

**You used to be pleasant and sweet to all of us,**
**But now you've turned into a huge GrumpaSaurus.**

**You yell and you scream for no reason at all.
Then smash your block buildings with your favorite ball.**

The nap that you missed helps to keep you calm,
So you don't get yelled at by your dad and your mom.

**Snack time was here and you sat by your plate,**
**Playing and doodling until it was late.**

**You didn't eat any food or drink any juice,**
**So your dad set you down and just let you loose.**

An hour went by, and your tummy started to grumble.
Then you yelled and you screamed and started to mumble.

"I'm hungry," you said with tears streaming down,
As you sniffled and pouted through your very long frown.

**Dinner was near, so no snack came about.**
**This led you to scream louder, and to jump and shout.**

**Your tummy grumbled more and you just couldn't cope…**

**Slowly you transformed into a big GrumpaLope.**

It's no fun to be hungry and grumpy all day.
Snack gives you energy to have fun and play.

**Play time was here and your sister was near,
You both grabbed some toys and started to cheer.**

But the toy that you got was one you didn't want,
So you dropped it right down and gave it a punt.

**The doll that your sister had was just what you needed.**
**You thought you could grab it and so you proceeded,**

**To take that toy doll without even caring.**
**Rather than try some talking and sharing.**

**You shoved her down, she took a big fall,**
**And your mom came right in and took all of the dolls.**

**Instead of apologizing you chased after us,
And you screamed and turned into a GrumpaPotamus.**

It's ok to be grumpy, but you should never be mean.
Don't take others' toys and then get mad and scream.

**Make sure to sleep well and get lots of rest,**
**So you don't get cranky and become a hot mess.**

**Eat your snack and stay clean, free from the grime,**
**Or else you will get an impromptu bath time.**

And if you refuse to be scrubbed by the sink,
You may just turn into the dreaded StinkaLink.

71358286R00018

Made in the USA
Columbia, SC
25 May 2017